Please, Take Yazz Home

(The Exciting Adventures of Yazz, the Stubborn Mule- Vol. #1)

Written & Created by

Dr. Queen Rogers, M.Ed.S.

Graphic Artwork Illustrations by Aniqa Ashfaq & Queen Rogers

All book proceeds will benefit Queens GEMS LLC (non-profit organization for girls)

For hardcover book sales or more information contact www.QueensGems.org or QueensGemsLLC@gmail.com

Visual Artwork & Text (2020) copyright © 2025 Queen Rogers

ISBN: 979-8-218-71098-9

Zo'rah

Bella

Yazz, the Mule

Brian

Skoinky

The exciting adventures of Yazz, the Stubborn Mule Vol. #1

Please, Take Yazz Home

Dedicated to my ALL students who love reading, my Queen's G.E.M.S. members, my nephews & nieces (Taylor, Noelle, Savannah, and the others), my children, and my children's "future" children (Aria & Aven).

"Hooray! Today is the big day, Zo'rah," declared Yazz, in a slow southern voice.

Little Skoinky quickly interrupted, "Oink, oink... Big day for what?"

Yazz replied, "Howdy Skoinky, it's the Queen's Town County Fair today!"

Skoinky responded, "Oh, I won first prize for the most unique animal last year.

I am half pig and half skunk. Zo'rah, you might win this year for being half horse and half zebra. Yazz, do you think you will win as half donkey and half horse?"

"I don't know," replied Yazz. "I'm just happy to leave the barnyard for the day."

"I guess I should start trotting towards the fair now. See you all later," uttered Yazz, the stubborn mule.

"Oh, no... perhaps he should wait for Brian and Bella," whispered Zo'rah.

Meanwhile, at the main house, bubbly Bella asked her younger, brave brother a question during breakfast. "Brian, do you think my Zo'rah or your stubborn mule is going to win first prize at the Queen's Town County Fair today?"

"I sure hope Yazz wins! I cleaned him up earlier this morning. What about Zo'rah the Zorse, your favorite Zebra-Horse," inquired Brian?

"My Zo'rah is ready to win first place," said Bella. The siblings continued to eat their healthy breakfast, as they both continued to dream about winning first prize at the fair.

Dad hollered out, "Oh, no!"

"What is it, dear?" Mom questioned with concern.

Dad read his newspaper aloud. "The Queen's Town County Fair is canceled today due to all the animals and people reportedly becoming very ill due to a serious virus. The entire town is requested to be quarantined (isolate/ stay home) until further notice."

"Dad, does this mean we are unable to take Yazz and Zo'rah to the County fair today?" asked Brian. Dad solemnly responded, "Yes, kids... The county fair is closed. We must remain safe and stay at home due to a serious virus."

The siblings asked to be excused from the breakfast table and ran outside to inform the animals in the barnyard.

Bella began to sob, "Sorry, guys... the fair is canceled today! The newspaper stated that we must stay home due to a virus."

Brian looked confused. "Where is Yazz?" he shouted.

All the animals pointed in the direction of the town. Bella and Brian both ran back towards the house to notify Mom and Dad.

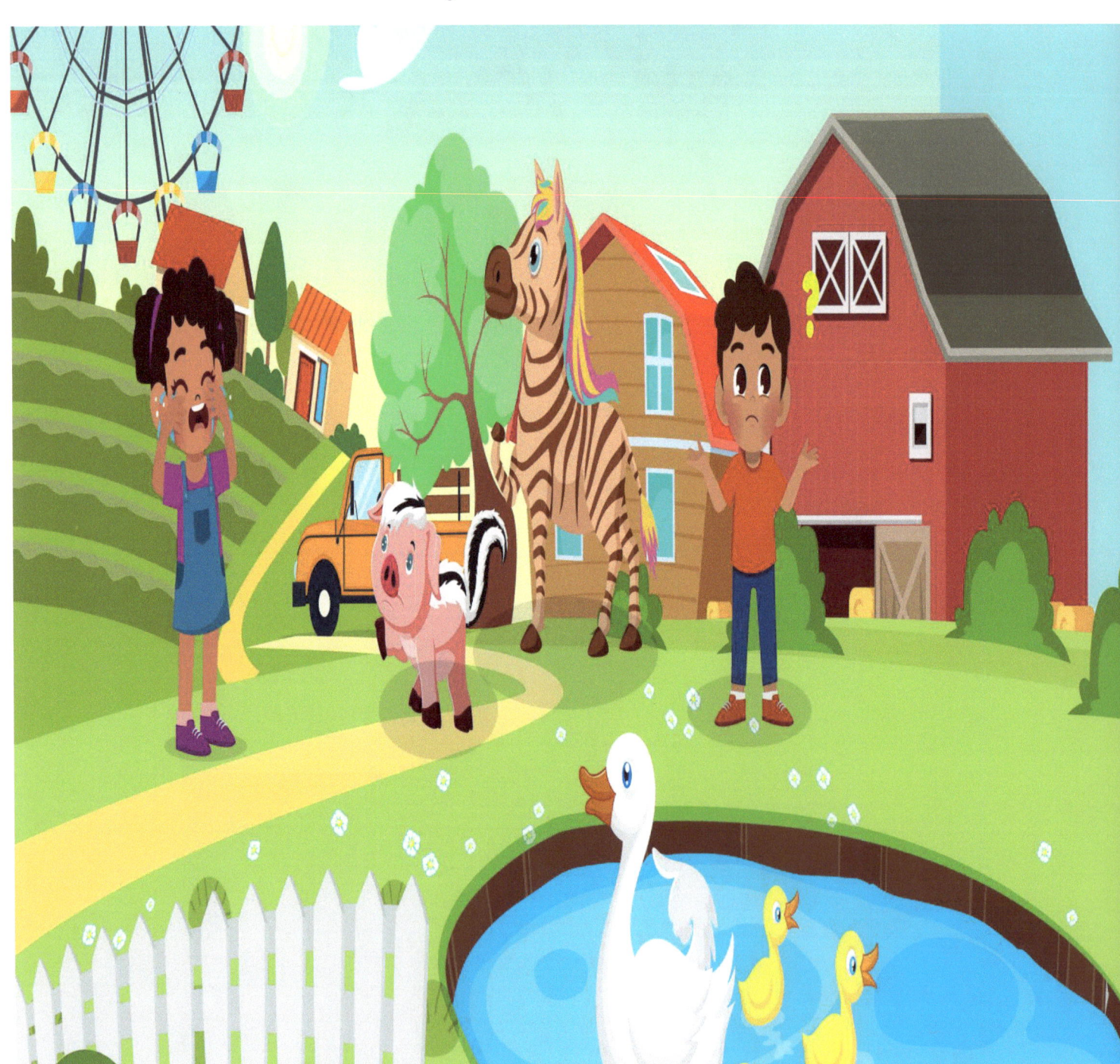

Yazz wandered around town, watching the shop owners close their stores.

He suddenly stopped and stood there, bewildered in front of Mr. Mel's Meat Store.

Mr. Mel walked outside and said, "Hola Yazzo... Where are Bella and Brian? You should not be out here alone. Go home now."

Yazz did not seem to understand as he continued trotting along towards the Queen's Town County Fair.

Brian and Bella's dad drove all around town looking for Yazz, their stubborn mule.

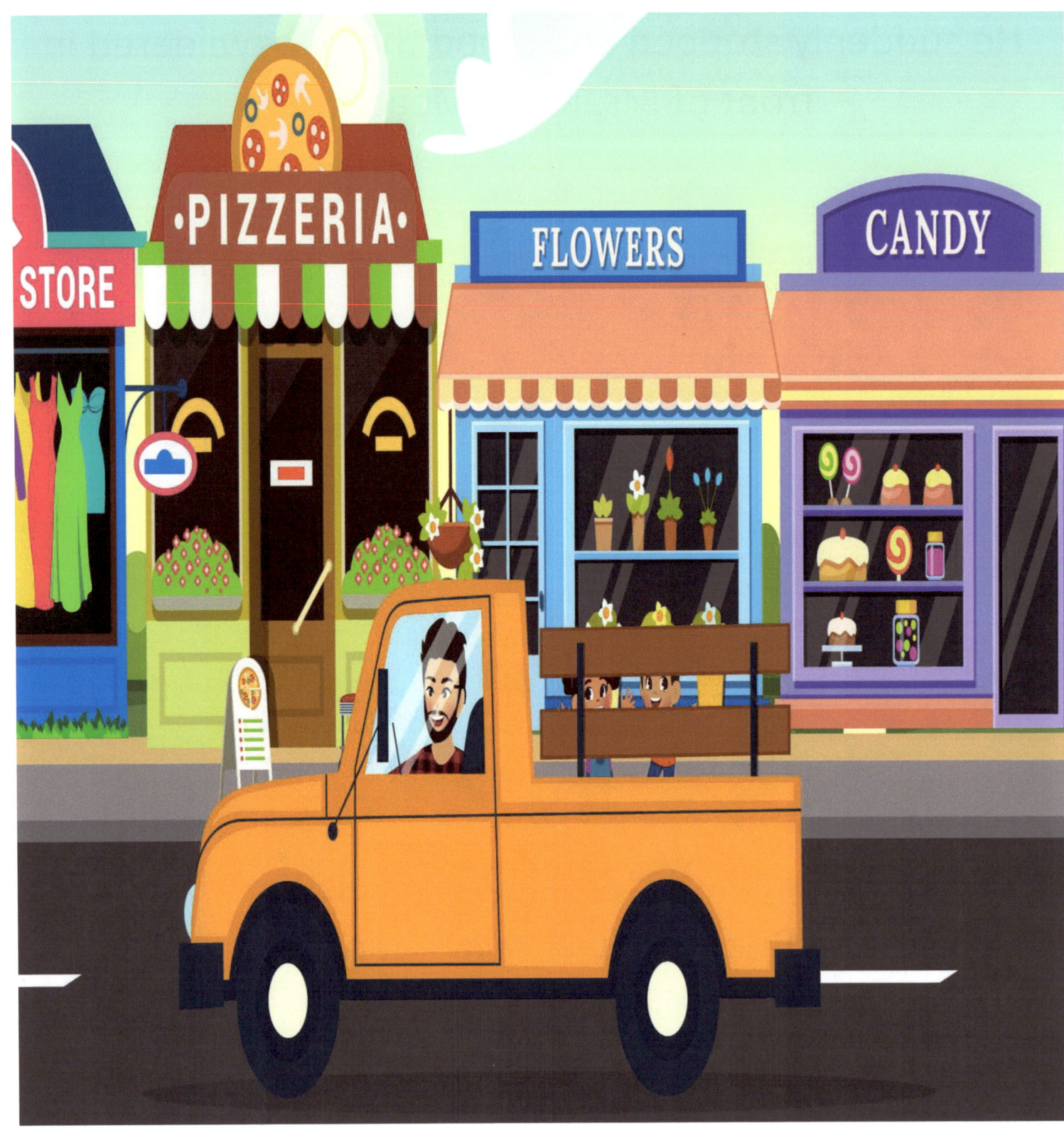

They saw Mr. Mel locking the front door of his meat shop. "Hello, Mr. Mel..." yelled Brian from the back of his dad's truck. "Have you seen Yazz today?"

"Yes, I did. Please take Yazz home as soon as you can. It's not safe," exclaimed Mr. Mel as he was pointing. "I think he went that way... towards the county fair."

Dad responded, "Thanks, Mr. Mel!" as he quickly drove off.

Brian bellowed loudly, "Dad, look! Yazz is walking towards the fair!"

Brian and Bella grabbed the rope as they jumped out of the truck. They pulled and shoved Yazz, but he stubbornly refused to move.

Suddenly, Officer Kase-Ali, Queen's Town Sheriff, came out wearing a mask. He stood near the front gate of the fair and yelled, "Please, take Yazz home! The fair is closed due to a serious virus." Yazz finally hopped in the back of Dad's truck.

Everyone seemed disappointed that the fair had to close due to a serious virus. However, they were all truly fortunate to be back home, safe at the barnyard.

"No School Tomorrow!"

The End

Draw a picture of your family below

Let's Review:

Why was the Queen's County Town Fair closed?

Which animal won last year for being the most unique animal?

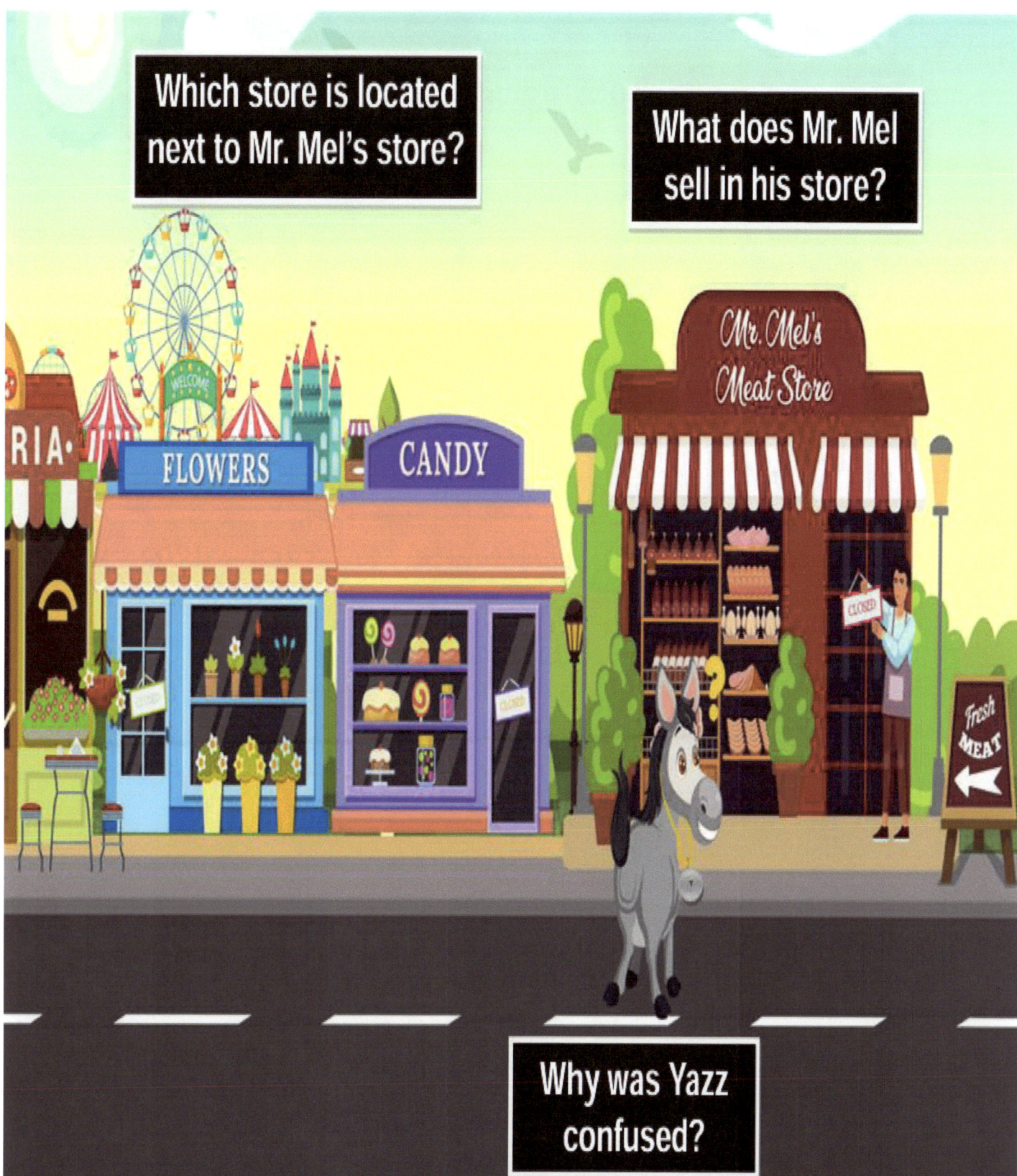

How many differences can you spot?